EGMONT
We bring stories to life

First published in Great Britain 2017 by Egmont UK Limited
The Yellow Building, 1 Nicholas Road, London W11 4AN

Written by Ned Hartley
Designed by Richie Hull and Glen Downey

© & ™ 2017 Lucasfilm Ltd.
ISBN 978 1 4052 8680 0
67213/1
Printed in the United Kingdom

To find more great *Star Wars* books, visit www.egmont.co.uk/starwars

WELCOME TO THE REBELLION

Warning! These are top secret data files, so be careful with them!

You now have access to the latest intel on the Rebel Alliance, as well as all the data on droids you'll ever need. You'll also find material on the greatest heroes and villains in the galaxy, so you can study their strengths and their weaknesses.

This information is very important, so please be careful with it.

Enter your name to begin...

NAME:	SPECIES:	HOMEWORLD:

CONTENTS

Star Wars TIMELINE

The whole history of *Star Wars!*

THE STORY BEGINS!
Anakin Skywalker meets Obi-Wan and Padmé.

RISE, LORD VADER
Anakin turns to the dark side. Obi-Wan and Anakin fight and Anakin becomes Darth Vader.

EVIL SPREADS
The evil Galactic Empire, lead by Emperor Palpatine, takes over the galaxy...

REBELS!
The crew of the *Ghost* fight back against the Empire.

32 BSW4   22 BSW4   19 BSW4   19 BSW4   19 BSW4   5 BSW4   0 BSW4

THE CLONE WARS
The Clone Wars rage on between clone troopers and the Separatist droid army.

IT'S TWINS
Padmé gives birth to Luke and Leia, who are hidden from Darth Vader.

GO ROGUE
Jyn Erso and her brave band of rebels are given a mission to steal the plans for the Death Star.

YOU ARE MY ONLY HOPE
Han Solo and Luke Skywalker save Princess Leia from the Empire.

JOIN ME
Darth Vader reveals to Luke that he is his father.

REDEEMED
Vader kills the Emperor, saving Luke, but dying in the process.

0 ASW4   3 ASW4   4 ASW4   34 ASW4

THERE HAS BEEN AN AWAKENING
Kylo Ren leads the First Order to take over the galaxy, but is stopped by Rey and the Resistance.

GREAT SHOT, KID!
Luke destroys the Death Star.

MEET THE REBELS

It's up to these brave freedom fighters to stop the evil Empire!

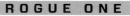

ROGUE ONE

CASSIAN ANDOR
Captain Andor is a rebel intelligence officer who is well respected in the Rebellion. He often knows more than he lets on, and is calm and collected under pressure.

JYN ERSO
Unpredictable and hot-tempered, Jyn has been on the run from the Empire since she was a child. She's tough and smart, but doesn't like working as part of a team.

CHIRRUT ÎMWE
Although Chirrut is blind he is attuned to the Force, which allows him to sense the battle around him.

K-2SO
Huge and imposing, this Imperial enforcer droid was reprogrammed and is now loyal to the rebel cause. He says what he thinks, even if that offends people!

10

BODHI ROOK
Bodhi was once an Imperial pilot but he was sent by Galen Erso with a special message for Jyn – he's trying to make up for his time working for the Empire.

BAZE MALBUS
Baze uses a heavy repeating blaster to battle the Empire. His blaster is powered by a compressed-gas cylinder which he wears on his back.

GALEN ERSO
Jyn's father is a brilliant scientist who tried to escape from the Empire, but they tracked him down and made him design a terrible weapon...

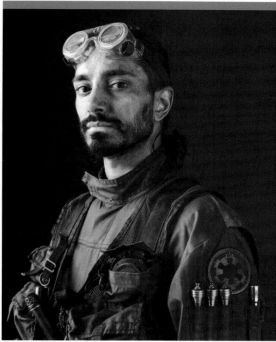

ALIENS

PAO
A platoon leader, Pao is a Drabatan commando who leads rebel forces into battle, shouting orders as he goes.

BISTAN
This Iakaru gunner loves to fire his heavy blaster out of the side of U-wings.

ADMIRAL RADDUS
Mon Calamari Officer (like Admiral Ackbar) who was one of the earliest opponents to the Empire. He commands the rebel fleet at the Battle of Scarif.

LEADERS

GENERAL DODONNA
Dodonna is in charge of the rebels' secret base on Yavin 4, which is the last, best hope against the Empire.

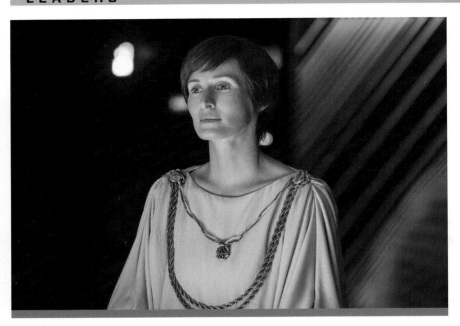

MON MOTHMA
Senator Mon Mothma worked for years in secret to fight the rise of the Emperor before becoming the leader of the Rebellion.

SAW GERRERA
Saw trained Jyn to fight the Empire. He leads a band of breakaway warriors against the Empire, but the Rebellion leaders think he is too extreme.

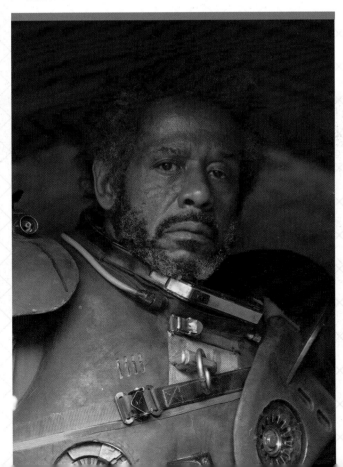

PRINCESS LEIA ORGANA
Even though she is younger than the other rebel leaders, Leia Organa fights just as hard for what is right.

GENERAL MERRICK
This brave pilot leads a team of starfighters under the call sign "Blue Leader".

WEDGE ANTILLES
Wedge was a former TIE fighter pilot before leaving the Empire and joining the rebels. He is a skilled X-wing pilot and joined Luke in Red Squadron.

LUKE SKYWALKER
As part of the X-wing Red Squadron Luke fired the proton torpedo that destroyed the Death Star.

HAN SOLO
Daring smuggler Han Solo didn't want to join the Rebellion at first, but he used his ship the *Millennium Falcon* to save Luke from Darth Vader.

BIGGS DARKLIGHTER
Luke Skywalker's childhood friend was an X-wing pilot in Red Squadron who died during the attack on the Death Star.

WHICH HERO ARE YOU?

If you joined the Rebel Alliance would you be brave like Luke, cunning like Han or tough like Jyn?
Answer these questions to find out!

1. Do you get in trouble for not following the rules?

☐ A. All the time!
☐ B. Only when I get caught!
☐ C. Never!

2. Do you make friends easily?

☐ A. Sometimes I can be a bit rude!
☐ B. Sure, I'm a charmer!
☐ C. I don't have that many friends my own age...

3. Do you like playing games?

☐ A. Not really.
☐ B. I love to gamble!
☐ C. Only for fun!

4. What do you do when someone is mean to you?

☐ A. Fight them!
☐ B. Say something rude back!
☐ C. Try to talk it out...

5. Do you long for adventure?

☐ A. I just want to do the right thing.
☐ B. I'd rather be rich!
☐ C. More than anything in the world!

6. Do you like to take risks?

☐ A. All the time!
☐ B. Only if there is money involved!
☐ C. Only if I *have* to.

7. What is the best thing about the Rebellion?

☐ A. Fighting the Empire!
☐ B. Making money!
☐ C. Action and adventure!

9. Are you good at telling people what to do?

- ☐ A. Yes, I'm quite inspiring!
- ☐ B. I can talk my way out of trouble. Sometimes.
- ☐ C. I like to teach people.

10. Have you ever stolen anything?

- ☐ A. Only when I had to.
- ☐ B. I might've cheated at cards once or twice...
- ☐ C. No, that would be wrong.

8. Who do you think is the most dangerous?

- ☐ A. Director Krennic
- ☐ B. Jabba the Hutt
- ☐ C. Darth Vader

WHO DID YOU CHOOSE?

Mostly As

You are JYN ERSO!
You're tough, but your real strength comes from those around you. Trust your friends and you can do amazing things!

Mostly Bs

You are HAN SOLO!
You're charming, but you're a bit of a rogue! Remember that you don't always have to be rewarded to do the right thing.

Mostly Cs

You are LUKE SKYWALKER!
You're very brave and you long for action and adventure! Study hard and there's no limit to what you could achieve!

X-WING PUZZLES!

The X-wing is one of the Rebel Alliance's greatest weapons against the Empire! Help the Rebellion by solving these puzzles.

FIX IT!

This X-wing was damaged in a dogfight with a TIE fighter. Work out where the missing pieces go, so it can fly again. Watch out, one piece doesn't fit on the X-wing . . .

DRAW A COOL HELMET DESIGN

You need a distinctive outfit if you're going to be an X-wing pilot. Draw a cool design on this helmet!

ATTACK!

Look through the cockpit of the X-wing! How many TIE fighters can you see?

A ◯__   B ◯__

C ◯__   D ◯__   E ◯__   F ◯__

NAVIGATE!

Which route should you take to get back to Yavin and not be hit by an asteroid?

YAVIN

GOOD JOB PILOT! YOU SAVED THE DAY!

START

1

EMPIRE: Your communications are disrupted. Miss a go.
2

3

FINISH!

26

25

REBELLION: TIE fighters attack! Go back one space.
24

23

STEAL THE DEATH STAR PLANS

Take it in turns to play as the rebels or the Empire!

PLAY THE GAME

- You need two players and one die. One player is the rebel team, the other plays as the Empire. Each player should have a counter.

- The rebels go first! If you need to, roll a dice and the player with the highest score can chose if they play as the rebels or the Empire.

- Take it in turns to roll the die and move your counter either backwards or forwards.

- Follow the instructions on the squares you land on, but only follow instructions for your team.

- If the Empire player lands on the rebel player's counter then the Empire wins the game. If the rebels get to the finish square then the rebels win!

EMPIRE: Fight Obi-Wan. Miss a go.
22

21

20

REBELLION: Rescue Princess Leia. Roll again.
19

18

4 ▶

REBELLION: U-wing support! Roll again. **5**

6 ▶

EMPIRE: Darth Vader arrives! Go forward one square. **7**

REBELLION: Hide the plans on a droid! Go forward two squares. **8**

9 ▼

10 ▼

EMPIRE: These aren't the droids you're looking for. Go back one square. **11**

12 ▼

EMPIRE: Blow up Alderaan! Roll again. **16**

17 ◀

15 ◀

REBELLION: Hide from the Empire. Miss a go. **14**

REBELLION: Hire Han Solo and the *Falcon*. Go forward a square. **13**

U-WING VERSUS TIE STRIKER

Which is better, the rebel gunship or the Imperial starfighter?

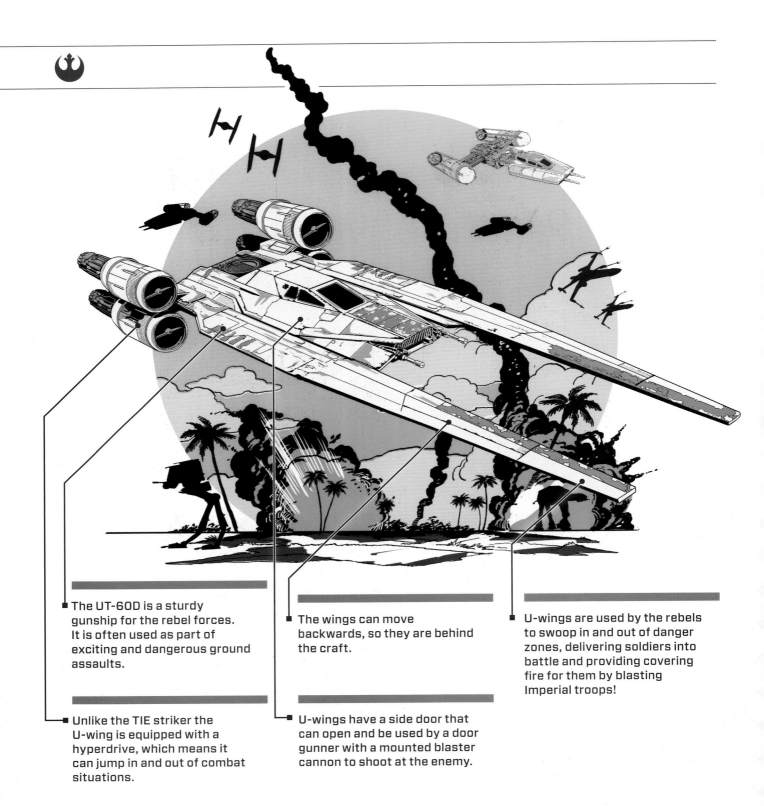

- The UT-60D is a sturdy gunship for the rebel forces. It is often used as part of exciting and dangerous ground assaults.

- Unlike the TIE striker the U-wing is equipped with a hyperdrive, which means it can jump in and out of combat situations.

- The wings can move backwards, so they are behind the craft.

- U-wings have a side door that can open and be used by a door gunner with a mounted blaster cannon to shoot at the enemy.

- U-wings are used by the rebels to swoop in and out of danger zones, delivering soldiers into battle and providing covering fire for them by blasting Imperial troops!

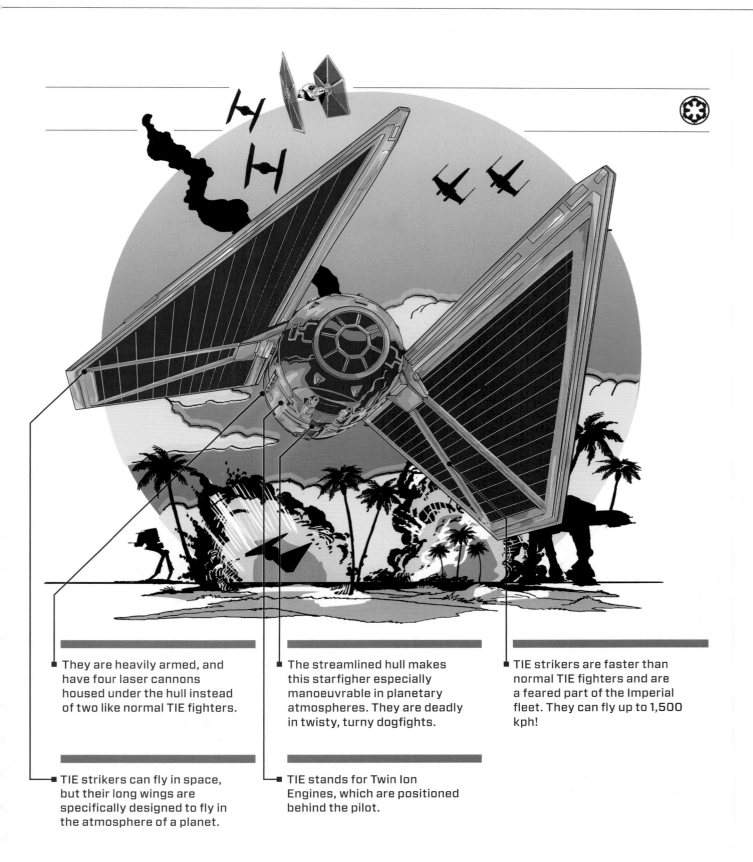

They are heavily armed, and have four laser cannons housed under the hull instead of two like normal TIE fighters.

The streamlined hull makes this starfigher especially manoeuvrable in planetary atmospheres. They are deadly in twisty, turny dogfights.

TIE strikers are faster than normal TIE fighters and are a feared part of the Imperial fleet. They can fly up to 1,500 kph!

TIE strikers can fly in space, but their long wings are specifically designed to fly in the atmosphere of a planet.

TIE stands for Twin Ion Engines, which are positioned behind the pilot.

WHERE'S THE WOOKIEE?

Chewbacca is being pursued by bounty hunters and has stowed away on Jabba's sail barge! Can you find him in this busy scene?

When you have found Chewbacca, see if you can spot Gungi and Rorjow!

See many more Wookiee hunts in the amazing *Where's the Wookiee?* activity books!

REBELLION CODES

Uncode these secret messages to help the Rebel Alliance!

A	ⴽ
B	ⴻ
C	ⵌ
D	ⵎ
E	ⵎ
F	ⵔ
G	ⵔ
H	ⵌ
I	ⵏ
J	ⵕ
K	ⵍ
L	ⵍ
M	ⵌ
N	△
O	△
P	ⵓ
Q	ⵔ
R	ⵌ
S	↓
T	↓
U	ⵓ
V	ⵢ
W	◻
X	△
Y	ⵎ
Z	ⵓ

WHAT ARE THESE HEROES TRYING TO SAY?

JEDHA IS

NOT SAFE

USE THE

FORCE

I HAVE THE

PLANS FOR THE

DEATH STAR

SPOT THE DIFFERENCE

Cassian has intercepted two images of Imperial troops, but one of them is a fake!
Can you spot SIX differences between the two pictures?

40 THINGS YOU DIDN'T KNOW ABOUT *STAR WARS*

To celebrate the fact that it's been 40 years since *Star Wars: A New Hope* hit cinemas, here are 40 exciting *Star Wars* facts!

FUNNY FACTS!

1 Look out for the stormtrooper bumping his head as he walks through a door in *Star Wars: A New Hope*! It happens just after Luke, Han and Leia get stuck in the trash compactor.

2 Someone says "I have a bad feeling about this" in every single *Star Wars* movie.

3 The *Millennium Falcon* has a pair of gold dice hanging in the cockpit - the ones Han Solo used to win the ship.

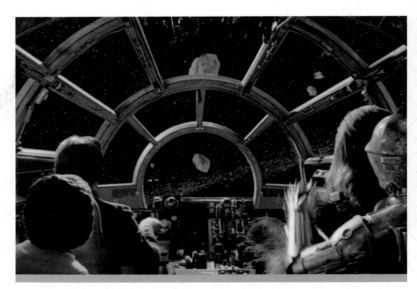

4 During the asteroid scene in *Empire Strikes Back*, one of the asteroids is actually a potato!

5 When Luke says "I can't see a thing in this helmet", that isn't a line in the script – actor Mark Hamill was really complaining that he couldn't see!

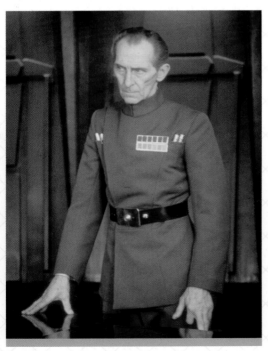

6 Actor Peter Cushing, who played Grand Moff Tarkin, wore carpet slippers for many scenes where his feet weren't visible. Why? Because his boots were too small and wouldn't fit!

7 The creepy creature in the trash compactor is called a dianoga – it eats rotting waste, and Luke Skywalker if it gets a chance!

9 No-one really knows what Jawas look like because they completely cover themselves, even their faces. They do know that Jawas smell really bad because they think washing is a waste of water! EW!

8 The blue milk Luke drinks comes from banthas, the elephant-like mounts that the Tusken Raiders ride.

10 Princess Leia calls Han Solo a "nerf herder". Nerfs are scruffy, smelly, surly beasts – and some people think their shepherds are too!

BEHIND THE SCENES

14 Almost no-one on the cast knew that Vader was Luke's father until the scene where Luke confronts Vader was filmed. Actor Mark Hamill only found out moments before.

11 The idea for the shape of the *Millennium Falcon* came from a hamburger with an olive next to it!

12 Actor Anthony Daniels couldn't sit down while wearing the C-3PO costume – they had to lean him against a board when he wasn't shooting his scenes!

13 The first C-3PO costume was so noisy and clanky that it was impossible to hear people talking. It also kept falling apart every few minutes.

15 Darth Vader's distinctive breathing was made by breathing through scuba diving gear.

16 Look behind the bar in the Mos Eisley cantina and you'll see the jet engine part that was later used for bounty hunter IG-88's head in *Empire Strikes Back*.

17 Things that were used to make the sounds of different aliens in *Star Wars: A New Hope*: Elephants, donkeys, bears and babies.

18 You can visit Luke's home and even stay there! The location where Skywalker home scenes were shot is the Sidi Driss Hotel in Tunisia.

BY THE NUMBERS

19 *Star Wars: A New Hope* has made over $775 million at the box office – it's one of the most successful films of all time.

20 C-3PO is fluent in six million forms of communication in *Return of the Jedi*, but by *The Force Awakens* he knows seven million. That's quite an upgrade!

21 There were 10,000 Jedi Knights in the Jedi Order, and nearly all were killed by Darth Vader and the Emperor!

22 The two suns on Tatooine are called Tatoo I and Tatoo II.

23 Darth Vader is only on screen for 12 minutes in *A New Hope*. It just feels like longer because he's so scary!

24 Chewbacca is over 200 years old... but it's OK, he's still young – Wookiees live for over 400 years.

25 Princess Leia is kept in detention cell 2187 on the Death Star. Finn's stormtrooper name is FN-2187; the same number!

WHO'S THAT?

29 Tusken Raiders believe that all water is sacred and promised to them, which is why they attack colonists.

30 Dewbacks, the large lizards ridden by sandtroopers, get their name because they lick the morning dew off their backs...

31 Chewbecca doesn't want to be handcuffed by Luke because it reminds him of his time as a slave to the Empire.

26 Boba Fett is a deadly bounty hunter who has weapons hidden all over his suit of armour, including vibroblades that come from his gauntlets and rocket dart launchers in his knee pads.

27 Other bounty hunters that Vader hires are mercenary Dengar, alien Zuckuss, and droids 4-LOM and IG-88.

28 Stormtrooper blaster rifles have a range of settings for different situations, including sting, stun and lethal force.

32 Chewbacca doesn't get a medal at the end of the film, even though Han and Luke do. Actor Peter Mayhew (in costume as Chewie) was given a medal as part of the 1997 MTV Movie Awards!

33 In *A New Hope* Jawas keep shouting "UTINNI!" which means "Come on!" or "Let's go!"

34 The hologram chess game that Chewie plays with C-3PO on the *Millennium Falcon* is called Dejarik. It's still working years later when Rey and Finn are on the *Falcon*.

35 The training remote that Luke uses to practise his lightsaber skills is still on the *Falcon*, too. Finn throws it out of his way when he's looking for bandages for Chewie!

36 Obi-Wan has a patch on his white robe just where it got burned in the battle with Anakin Skywalker in *Revenge of the Sith*.

37 The X-wings used by Poe and the Resistance in *The Force Awakens* are different from the ones in *A New Hope*. Look at their engines!

38 When Rey touches Luke's lightsaber she has a vision and hears the voices of Yoda and Obi-Wan. The Force is strong with her!

39 Luke was originally going to be called "Luke Starkiller", but it was changed to "Luke Skywalker". That's where the name "Starkiller Base" comes from.

40 Yoda's hut on Dagobah isn't just built from mud and stones, part of it is built from the escape pod that brought him to the planet.

COOLEST DROIDS EVER

These mechanical marvels are magnificent!

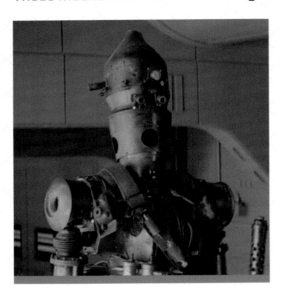

IG-88
A dangerous Assassin droid who worked as a bounty hunter – IG-88 was so deadly that Darth Vader sent him to find Han Solo. Sadly for IG-88 his rival Boba Fett managed to get to Han first!
Weapons: Heavy pulse cannon, poison darts, toxic gas dispensers, vibroblades

R2-D2
This feisty astromech droid has been everywhere! R2 helped blow up the Death Star, witnessed Padmé and Anakin's wedding and later helped piece together the map to find Luke Skywalker. He normally hangs out with his friend C-3PO, even though they spend most of their time arguing!
Weapons: Electroshock prod, utility arm, buzz saw, fusion welder.

K-2SO
This massive Enforcer Droid was created by the Empire, but captured and reprogrammed by the Rebellion. He served Captain Cassian Andor and was part of the daring mission to steal the plans for the Death Star!
Weapons: None

Probe Droids
These clever droids were sent all over the galaxy by Darth Vader to find the secret location of the rebel base. The one sent to Hoth wasn't quick enough to avoid Han Solo's blaster fire though!
Weapons: Blaster, Self-destruct mechanism

Battle Droids
The B1 battle droids were the most common droids in the Droid Army. What they lack in intelligence they make up for in sheer numbers – charging at their enemies trying to overwhelm them.
Weapons: Blaster rifle, thermal detonators

BB-8
Poe Dameron's astromech is one of the most loyal and brave droids in the galaxy. He proved he was a hero by keeping the location of Luke Skywalker safe from the First Order and delivering it to the Resistance!
Weapons: Electroshock prod, welding torch.

Droideka
Even the Jedi have a hard time taking these guys down! They've got huge blasters, energy shields that can even deflect lightsaber attacks, and they can transform into a ball to roll in and out of battle quickly.
Weapons: Twin blaster cannons, shield generator

C-3PO
He knows seven million forms of communication, but his favourite thing to do is complain! C-3PO was built out of spare parts by Anakin Skywalker and travelled the galaxy with his friend and counterpart R2-D2. Most recently he has joined the Resistance with General Leia and has a new red arm (which he doesn't like).
Weapons: None.

ASTROMECH MATCHING

Every X-wing pilot needs an astromech droid! Yours is the one that DOESN'T have an identical partner. Which one is it?

DRAW C-3PO

Want to learn how to draw the golden protocol droid? Just copy this picture into the grid on the right!

C-3PO

Type: Protocol Droid
Model: 3PO unit
Manufacturer: Cybot Galactica
Height: 1.67m
Function: Translation; human-cyborg relations
Equipment: TranLang III communication module
Notes: The latest versions of the translation module support over 7 million languages

FIX R2-D2

R2-D2 has taken a beating from the Jawas! Solve these puzzles to help Luke get him working again!

WHO'S THAT?

R2's photoreceptor is damaged and all the images are blurry!
Can you work out who is in these pictures?

 Leia

 Ben Kenobi

 Darth Vader

Type: Astromech Droid
Model: R2 unit
Manufacturer: Industrial Automaton
Height: 1.09m
Function: Copilot; starship mechanic
Equipment: Holoprojector; data probe; buzz saw; rocket booster
Notes: R2 units contain many kinds of useful tools for starship repair

BROKEN CONNECTIONS

Luke needs to rewire R2's power unit so that it has the least resistance. Which route should he take so that all the numbers add up to the lowest possible number? Go from point to point, adding the numbers as you go. What's the lowest number you can get?

IGNITION SEQUENCE

Help R2 get booted up again by working out what comes next in these sequences.

1 2 3

BB-8 BLUEPRINTS

Peek inside the bravest little droid in the Resistance!

BB-8 speaks a version of the droid language of Binary. Poe and Rey both speak it, but Finn doesn't have a clue what BB-8 is saying!

TOP VIEW   BOTTOM VIEW

BB-8

Type: Astromech Droid
Model: BB unit
Manufacturer: [data missing]
Height: 0.67m
Function: Copilot; starship mechanic
Equipment: Arc welder; holoprojector; liquid cable launchers
Notes: The heads of BB units stay attached using powerful magnets

INTERGALACTIC ARRAY

BB-8 is designed to fit in the back of Poe's T-70 X-wing starfighter.

HOLOGRAPHIC PROJECTOR

ACCELEROMETERS

ORIENTATION SENSORS

SYSTEM VENTILATION

PENTA-DRIVE CASTERS

DROID MATRIX

K-2SO's droid brain contains detailed files on the rebel mission to investigate the Empire's new superweapon. To decode them, find the words in the matrix below. The letters that are left will spell out a secret message...

WORDS TO FIND

- ANDOR
- BAZE
- BODHI
- CASSIAN
- CHIRRUT
- DRAVEN
- EADU
- EMPIRE
- ERSO
- GALEN
- GENERAL
- GERRERA
- ÏMWE
- JEDHA
- JYN
- KAFRENE
- KRENNIC
- MALBUS
- ORSON
- REBELS
- ROOK
- SAW
- TARKIN
- WOBANI
- YAVIN

T	T	H	E	K	E	D	W	E	A	T	H	S
T	U	A	O	R	R	P	U	A	L	B	G	A
N	R	O	S	A	I	C	D	L	S	O	E	R
E	R	L	C	O	P	C	A	L	R	D	R	A
A	I	T	I	E	M	R	E	S	D	H	R	W
I	H	N	N	A	E	B	O	T	S	I	E	O
H	C	D	N	N	E	N	E	I	I	I	R	B
T	M	D	E	R	S	O	P	E	M	R	A	A
A	O	G	R	J	I	A	L	N	W	Z	A	N
R	R	N	K	A	F	R	E	N	E	C	H	I
K	I	V	Y	A	V	I	N	E	O	L	N	T
I	H	E	P	J	L	E	S	U	B	L	A	M
N	A	N	E	T	S	C	N	A	R	I	F	G

K-2SO

Type: Enforcer Droid
Model: KX unit
Manufacturer: Arkayd Industries
Height: 2.16m
Function: Defence; escort duties; security
Equipment: Computer interface arm; communication package
Notes: KX software is hardened against unauthorised reprogramming

VADER'S MOST POWERFUL MOMENTS

The dark lord of the Sith is one of the strongest warriors in the galaxy!

Admiral Ozzel
Darth Vader didn't even need to be in the same part of the spaceship as this incompetent Admiral to attack him. When Admiral Ozzel pulled out of hyperspace too close to the rebel base on Hoth Vader was not pleased! Vader used the Force to reach out across the ship and punish him...

Obi-Wan Kenobi
When Darth Vader and Obi-Wan faced off on the Death Star, Vader hadn't seen his old master for nearly twenty years. After a fierce lightsaber battle, Obi-Wan turned off his lightsaber and Darth Vader struck him down!

Capturing Han Solo
Han Solo fired his blaster on Vader on Cloud City, but Vader was able to deflect the blasts using the Force. Don't mess with Darth Vader!

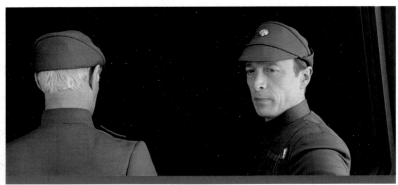

Captain Needa
The brave Captain Needa travelled to Vader's Star Destroyer to personally apologise for failing to capture the *Millennium Falcon*. Darth Vader did accept Captain Needa's apology – but only after his death.

The Battle of Yavin
While rebels attacked the Death Star, Vader proved once again that he is an amazing fighter pilot, shooting down X-wings and Y-wings from his modified TIE advanced. He was stopped when he was bashed out of position by Han Solo in the *Millennium Falcon*.

Ending The Emperor
Vader's last act was perhaps his most noble one. Even though he was hurt in a lightsaber battle he used his last remaining energy to throw Emperor Palpatine into the Death Star's reactor and save Luke's life!

STORMTROOPERS OF THE EMPIRE

The galaxy is a huge place and the Empire needs lots of different types of trooper to adapt to the different environments. Can you tell them apart?

TANK TROOPER

These troopers are military crew for hover tanks that patrol Empire-occupied worlds like Jedha. They have lighter leg armour so they can get in and out of their hover tanks quickly.

STORMTROOPER

The standard rank and file soldiers of the Empire wear white armour which strikes fear in the hearts of citizens. While their armour is strong it offers little protection against a direct blaster hit.

DEATH TROOPER

These specialised soldiers are the elite troops of Imperial Military Intelligence, and the personal bodyguards and enforcers of Director Orson Krennic. Their black armour makes them stand out against other Empire forces.

SHORETROOPER

Specialised armour allows these troopers greater manoeuvrability for aquatic defence. They patrol the beaches and bunkers of the Imperial military headquarters on the tropical planet Scarif.

SNOWTROOPER

Icy worlds like Hoth need special troopers – their armour is insulated and heated against the cold, their helmet have snow goggles and they even have their own homing beacons in case they get lost in the snow.

SANDTROOPER

When the Empire needs to patrol desert worlds like Tatooine they send sandtroopers. Their armour contains cooling fans and their helmet holds a sand filter. Plus, their survival backpack holds rations and water – just in case!

SCOUT TROOPER

These lightly armed troops are best for exciting missions like reconnaissance and infiltration. Scout troopers rode speeder bikes on the forest moon of Endor while protecting the shield generator for the second Death Star.

WEAPONS

Standard issue armaments for the Empire's loyal soldiers!

E-11 blaster rifle

This standard issue weapon is manufactured by BlasTech Industries, lethal on the battlefield.

DLT-19 heavy blaster riffle

A much heavier weapon, the DLT-19 has a higher rate of fire and is effective at longer range. It's very useful against large groups of enemies.

Thermal detonator

An incredibly powerful explosive device, which can be set to a short timer. Princess Leia Organa used one to "negotiate" a deal with Jabba the Hutt.

ESCAPE THE EMPIRE!

Jyn is being chased through Jedha. Can you help her escape? If you make a wrong choice you'll get to a dead end!

NO

Cassian is wounded. Leave him?

YES

Let K-2SO talk you past a patrol?

NO

YES

NO

Saw's rebels are here. Let them help?

YES

NO

YES

A scout walker! Try to sneak past?

FINISH!

You've made it to the U-wing and have escaped! Well done!

47

KRENNIC'S COMMANDS

Solve these puzzles, sent directly from the desk of the director of Advanced Weapons Research!

Orson Krennic is the Director of the Imperial Military's Advanced Weapons Research division. He is a proud, unpredictable and ruthless man with a thirst for power, and will stop at nothing to win favour with the Emperor.

Krennic is a member of the secret Tarkin Initiative think-tank, which designs terrifying superweapons; he is guarded by elite Death Troopers, who can be recognised by their distinctive black armour and advanced equipment.

DEATH TROOPER
This image of death troopers has been scrambled. Put the sections in the right order to repair the Imperial file.

1. B
2. D
3. A
4. C
5. E

A

B

C

D

E

48

BY THE NUMBERS

Director Krennic runs many secret weapons research projects – including the construction of the dreaded Death Star. Can you fit all of these special projects into the Imperial Archive's data library?

WORDS TO FIT

STELLAR SPHERE

MARK OMEGA

PAX AURORA

WAR MANTLE

CLUSTER PRISM

BLACK SABER

STARDUST

THE COOLEST LIGHTSABERS

Every Jedi needs to be able to recognise a warrior by his lightsaber – here are some of the greatest ones ever made!

LIGHT SIDE

LUKE SKYWALKER
Luke lost his first lightsaber after Darth Vader chopped his hand off – OUCH! But as soon as he got a replacement robot hand he made himself a new lightsaber.

MACE WINDU
It's always easy to spot Mace Windu in a crowd of Jedi with his supercool purple lightsaber.

YODA
Everything about Jedi Master Yoda is small, so it makes sense that his lightsaber is tiny too. The only thing that isn't small is his ability to use it!

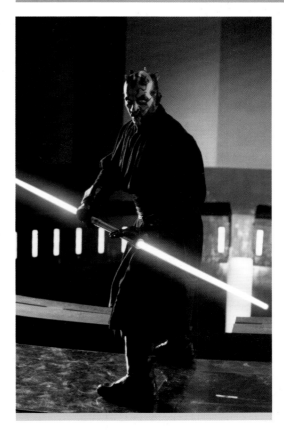

DARTH MAUL
This double-ended lightsaber meant that Darth Maul could fight two Jedi at the same time!

DARTH VADER
Rebels across the galaxy are terrified of Darth Vader's distinctive red lightsaber!

KYLO REN
The crossguard makes it look different, but the coolest thing about this lightsaber is how fiery and wild it is. Just like its owner!

LIGHTSABER TRAINING

Lightsaber combat takes many years to master. Each strike has to flow naturally from the one before it, guided by the Force. Use your Jedi skills to complete the following training sequences.

1   **2**   **3**   **4**   **5**   **6**

LIGHTSABER CONSTRUCTION

To compete your Jedi skills you will need to build your own lightsaber! Sketch its design below, using these famous weapons to inspire you.

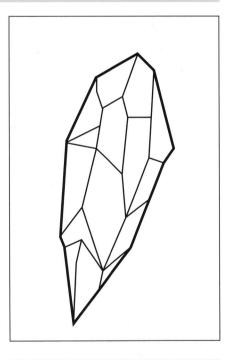

Don't forget to colour in the kyber crystal that will power your blade with the colour you prefer.

HOW TO BE A JEDI

Ever wanted to be a warrior for peace, patrolling the galaxy with your trusty lightsaber? Here are some tips for making that happen!

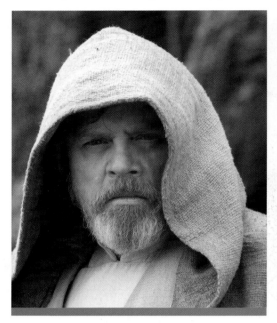

It's all in the Family
The Force is strong in Luke Skywalker's family and maybe it is in your family too! Are any of your relatives Jedi? You should probably ask them.

Dress for success
Jedi wear loose-fitting clothes that don't restrict their movement while fighting or performing acrobatic feats.

Train, train, train!
Can you move objects using only your mind? Or you could just do the puzzles in this Annual – that counts as training!

Face your fear...
Part of Jedi training is facing the thing that your fear the most. For Luke it was Darth Vader, what are YOU most scared of?

... But don't be afraid
As Master Yoda explains to Luke Skywalker, "Fear is the path to the dark side. Fear leads to anger. Anger leads to hate. Hate leads to suffering."

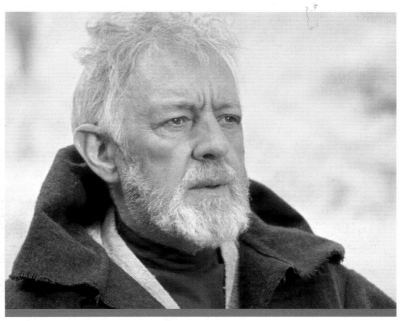

Be brave and noble
A Jedi always tries to do the right thing, and help people around them. The light side of the Force is about being good!

You might have to wait a while
Obi-Wan waited on Tatooine for Luke for nearly 20 years. You need to be patient to be a Jedi!

Learn new things
Knowledge is very important to becoming a Jedi. Make sure you spend time with new books learning things!

Make a lightsaber
An important part of Jedi training is making your own lightsaber. First, you will need to find yourself a kyber crystal, though ...

Keep calm
Things don't always go your way. Don't get too frustrated or you could end up like Anakin and go to the dark side.

REY: SCAVENGER!

Rey spent years living on Jakku on her own before she zoomed off on a life of adventure.

HOW TO SURVIVE

As a child Rey was left on the desert planet of Jakku. She spent years waiting on Jakku for her family to come back for her. She learned to fend for herself and survive by scavenging old technology. A huge battle between the Empire and the Rebellion took place on Jakku before Rey was born, and the planet is littered with crashed ships.

HOW TO MAKE A HOME

Rey made a home in a crashed Imperial AT-AT called the Hellhound Two. She slowly made it feel like a proper home, and marked the passage of time with scratches on the wall.

HOW TO EAT

Traders like Unkar Plutt will swap scavenged weapons and technology for food. Most of the food was left over rations from New Republic or Imperial soldiers.

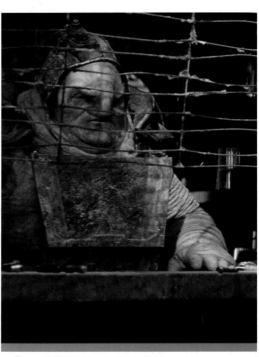

HOW TO GET AROUND

She built herself a speeder out of bits she found from other craft, including repulsorlifts taken from crashed X-wings. It's so fast and top-heavy that only a skilled driver like Rey can pilot it.

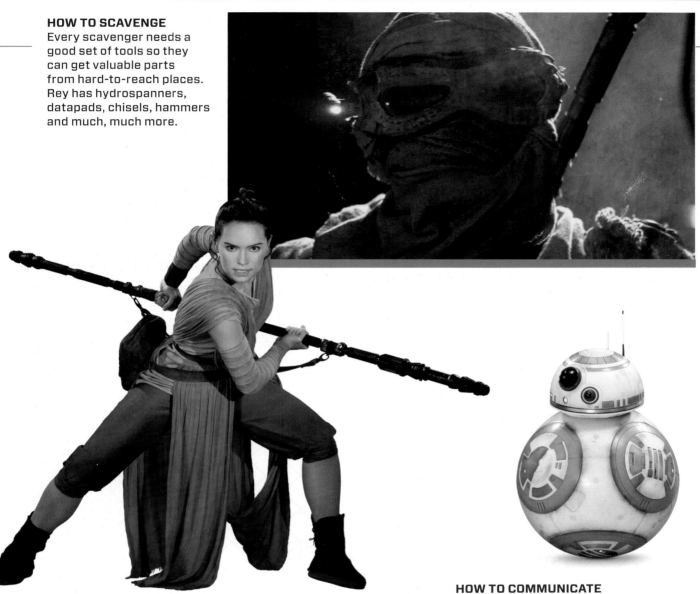

HOW TO SCAVENGE
Every scavenger needs a good set of tools so they can get valuable parts from hard-to-reach places. Rey has hydrospanners, datapads, chisels, hammers and much, much more.

HOW TO FIGHT
On Niima Outpost on Jakku, Rey was well known for being able to defend herself with a quarterstaff. She taught herself how to use her staff to smack down lots of enemies at the same time!

HOW TO COMMUNICATE
In her spare time Rey practised speaking alien languages and even the languages of droids. That was how she was able to talk to BB-8 when she first met him.

HOW TO GET OFF JAKKU
Rey spent years waiting for someone to come and get her and take her from Jakku. While she was waiting she set up a computer inside her AT-AT home so she could run flight simulations flying different starfighters; which is why she was able to fly the *Millennium Falcon* so well when she got in the cockpit.

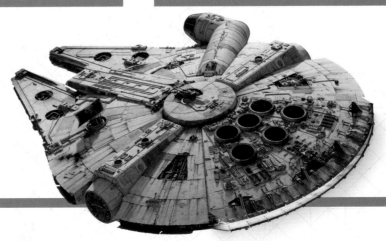

FINN: STORMTROOPER!

Before he was a hero of the Resistance, Finn was a solider in the First Order.

RAISED BY THE FIRST ORDER
Finn was a taken from his family by the First Order when he was so young that he doesn't even remember them. The First Order trained him, and made him into a powerful soldier.

NO NAME
He was given the name FN-2187 by the First Order, and his stormtrooper friends called him "Eight-Seven". When Poe met Finn he refused to call him FN-2187, giving him the new name of Finn instead.

WEAPONS MASTER
Finn knows how to use a blaster, but doesn't want to use his training to hurt innocent people. He's scared of the powerful might of the First Order, and he knows how ruthless they are.

SOMETHING SMELLS!
He was put in a unit with other stromtroopers and watched closely by Captain Phasma. Captain Phasma can't have been too impressed, because she put him in charge of the toilets on Starkiller Base!

TRAITOR!
One of Finn's stormtrooper friends was FN-2199, who was called "Nines" by the other stromtroopers. Nines was upset when Finn deserted the First Order, and attacked Finn with a Z6 riot control baton when he saw him at Takodana.

POE DAMERON: ACE PILOT!

He's the greatest pilot in the Resistance, and the coolest one too.

ALL IN THE FAMILY
Poe's mother was also a pilot and fought in the battle of Endor! She taught him how to fly her old A-wing.

BEST OF THE BEST
Poe leads an elite squadron of X-wings under the callsign "Black Leader". All X-wings in his squadron have been painted black to make them stand out against other starfighters.

BB-8'S MATE!
BB-8 is Poe's astromech droid, fitting neatly into his X-wing. Poe and BB-8 have been on lots of adventures together and trust each other with their lives.

TRUSTED OPERATIVE
General Leia gives the most dangerous and sensitive missions to Poe. No matter how hard the job, she knows Poe won't let her down.

FLYBOY
Poe can fly pretty much anything. He could work out how to fly a TIE fighter within minutes of sitting down at the controls. Smart!

ANSWERS

pg 16. X-WING PUZZLES
A. x B. x C. x D. x E. x F. x
How many TIE fighters can you see?
X
Which route should you take? 2

pg 24 REBELLION CODES
Jedha is not safe
Use the force
I have the plans for the Death Star

pg 25 SPOT THE DIFFERENCE

pg 34 R2-D2 MATCH

pg 36 -37 FIX R2-D2

 LEIA
 BEN KENOBI
 DARTH VADER

pg 40-41 DROID MATRIX

T	T	H	E	K	E	D	W	E	A	T	H	S
T	U	A	O	R	R	P	U	A	L	B	G	A
N	R	O	S	A	I	C	D	L	S	O	E	R
E	R	L	C	O	P	C	A	L	R	D	R	A
A	I	T	I	E	M	R	E	S	D	H	R	W
I	H	N	N	A	E	B	O	T	S	I	E	O
H	C	D	N	N	E	N	E	I	I	I	R	B
T	M	D	E	R	S	O	P	E	M	R	A	A
A	O	G	R	J	I	A	L	N	W	Z	A	N
R	R	N	K	A	F	R	E	N	E	C	H	I
K	I	V	Y	A	V	I	N	E	O	L	N	T
I	H	E	P	J	L	E	S	U	B	L	A	M
N	A	N	E	T	S	C	N	A	R	I	F	G

pg 46-47 ESCAPE THE EMPIRE

IGNITION SEQUENCE

pg 48-49 KRENNIC'S COMMANDS

1. B
2. D
3. A
4. C
5. E

pg 52 LIGHTSABER TRAINING